Amanda and the Witch Switch

Amanda and the Witch Switch

Story and Pictures by
John Himmelman

PUFFIN BOOKS

PUFFIN BOOKS
Published by the Penguin Group
A division of Penguin Books USA Inc.,
375 Hudson Street, New York, New York 10014, U.S.A.
Penguin Books Ltd, 27 Wrights Lane, London W8 5TZ, England
Penguin Books Australia Ltd, Ringwood, Victoria, Australia
Penguin Books Canada Ltd, 10 Alcorn Avenue, Toronto, Ontario, Canada M4V 3B2
Penguin Books (N.Z.) Ltd, 182–190 Wairau Road, Auckland 10, New Zealand

Penguin Books Ltd, Registered Offices: Harmondsworth, Middlesex, England

First published by Viking Penguin Inc. 1985
Published in Picture Puffins 1987
7 9 10 8 6
Copyright © John Himmelman, 1985
All rights reserved

Set in Bookman Light

Library of Congress Cataloging in Publication Data
Himmelman, John.   Amanda and the witch switch.
Reprint. Originally published: New York, N.Y., U.S.A.: Viking Kestrel, 1985.
Summary: A friendly witch named Amanda gives a
toad three wishes, but her good intentions backfire
when he uses one of them to become a witch.
[1. Witches—Fiction. 2. Toads—Fiction] I. Title.
PZ7.H5686Am   1987   [E]   86-16936   ISBN 0-14-050635-7

*This book is dedicated to Mom,
and to my fond memories
of Grandma Nault.*

Up in the hills,

deep in the forest,

there lived a friendly old witch.
Her name was Amanda.

One morning while she was rocking
in her chair, she decided it was too
lovely a day to spend indoors.

Amanda stepped outside and stretched.
"What a beautiful day it is," she said.
"Today I will do something extra nice!"

She added some flowers here and there,

taught some beavers how to boogie,

and some trees how to sing,

but that still didn't seem like enough.

Then she came upon a little toad
sitting on a rock.

"My name is Amanda," she said,
"and it is such a nice day today
that I will make three of your wishes
come true."

"Okay," said the toad.

"Make me a prince."

"Sorry, I can only do that for frogs,"
she answered.

"All right then," said the toad.
"Make me a witch, like yourself."
Amanda thought for a moment.
"Well, I suppose I could," and *POOF!*

The toad turned into a witch!

Then the toad pointed to Amanda.

"And now I want *you* to turn into a toad."

and *POOF!*
Amanda was turned into a toad.

Amanda sat there *looking* helpless
as the toad went off into the forest.
"Now I can do any magic I want," he said.

He turned a pond into mud,

made a deer's antlers into flowers,

turned some rocks into marshmallows,

and made some rabbits turn purple.

He made a bear the size of a bee

and a bee the size of a bear.

But this last prank backfired,
and the bee went after the toad!

I'll just turn myself back into a toad
and threaten to eat him if he doesn't
put me down, he thought.

But this didn't quite work out the way
he planned.

"*Help,*" he called to Amanda.

"*Please help me!*"

I guess he's learned his lesson,
thought Amanda, and she turned the bee
back to normal size.

"Well, you still have one more wish,"
she said to the toad.

"I wish everything was back
the way it was," he said.

"I thought you would," said Amanda,
and she turned everything back to normal.

Well, almost everything.